Dear Parent:
Your child's love of reading ~~start~~ ~~here~~

Every child learns to read in a different way and at his or her own speed. Some go back and forth between reading levels and read favorite books again and again. Others read through each level in order. You can help your young reader improve and become more confident by encouraging his or her own interests and abilities. From books your child reads with you to the first books he or she reads alone, there are I Can Read Books for every stage of reading:

SHARED READING
Basic language, word repetition, and whimsical illustrations, ideal for sharing with your emergent reader

BEGINNING READING
Short sentences, familiar words, and simple concepts for children eager to read on their own

READING WITH HELP
Engaging stories, longer sentences, and language play for developing readers

READING ALONE
Complex plots, challenging vocabulary, and high-interest topics for the independent reader

ADVANCED READING
Short paragraphs, chapters, and exciting themes for the perfect bridge to chapter books

I Can Read Books have introduced children to the joy of reading since 1957. Featuring award-winning authors and illustrators and a fabulous cast of beloved characters, I Can Read Books set the standard for beginning readers.

A lifetime of discovery begins with the magical words **"I Can Read!"**

Visit www.icanread.com for information
on enriching your child's reading experience.

HarperCollins®, ✹®, and I Can Read Book® are trademarks of HarperCollins Publishers.

Ice Age: Dawn of the Dinosaurs: All in the Family
Ice Age: Dawn of the Dinosaurs ™ & © 2009 Twentieth Century Fox Film Corporation.
All Rights Reserved. Manufactured in China.
No part of this book may be used or reproduced in any manner whatsoever without written permission
except in the case of brief quotations embodied in critical articles and reviews. For information address
HarperCollins Children's Books, a division of HarperCollins Publishers, 10 East 53rd Street, New York, NY 10022.
www.icanread.com

Library of Congress Catalog card number: 2008942547
ISBN 978-0-06-168977-2

Typography by Rick Farley
13 SCP 10 9 8 7 6 5 4

❖

First Edition

ICE AGE™
DAWN OF THE DINOSAURS

ALL IN THE FAMILY

Adapted by Sierra Harimann

HarperCollinsPublishers

Manny was excited.

He was going to be a dad.

Ellie was Manny's wife.

She was going to have a baby.

Their family of mammoths

was about to grow.

Ellie and Manny lived
during the Ice Age
with all of their friends.
Their friends were family, too.
Crash and Eddie the possums
were excited about the baby.

So was Sid the sloth.

But Diego the saber-toothed tiger

wasn't sure how he felt.

One day,

Manny wanted to surprise Ellie

with a gift.

He invited everyone to see it.

"Can I look now?" asked Ellie.

"Now!" said Manny.

Manny had made a pretty mobile
from the ice crystal.
Manny, Ellie, and the baby
were on the mobile.
"It's our family," said Manny.
"It's amazing," said Ellie.

Just then, Ellie felt the baby move.

"What's happening?" said Manny.

"Are you having the baby?

Take a deep breath.

Nobody else breathe!"

"It was just a kick," said Ellie.

"Manny, you've got to relax,"
said Ellie.
"The best way to protect our baby
is to have our friends around us."
Then Ellie realized something.
Where was Diego?

Diego was far away,

chasing a gazelle.

Diego was not thinking about babies.

He did not care about mobiles.

Diego wanted a life of adventure.

When Diego finally showed up,
he told Manny how he felt.
"I'm happy for you," he said,
"but having a family is
your adventure, not mine."

"It might be time for me
to head out on my own," said Diego.
Manny was hurt.
He thought Diego didn't want to be
part of the family anymore.

"Well, go find some adventure,
Mr. Adventure Guy," said Manny.
"Don't let my boring life
hit you on the way out."

Sid tried to stop Diego from going.

"We're a herd. A family!" he said.

"Things have changed," said Diego.

Diego didn't think anything
could make him stick around.
But when he heard
that the baby was on its way,
something inside him changed.

Diego wanted to be there for Ellie.
He wanted to celebrate with Sid,
Manny, and all of his friends.
Maybe having a baby in the family
would be its own great adventure.

Soon, the baby was born.

It was a girl!

"Welcome to the Ice Age, sweetie,"
said Ellie.

"She's beautiful," Sid said.

"I'm glad she looks like Ellie.

No offense, Manny."

"Thanks for coming back,"
Manny told Diego.
"I know this baby stuff
isn't for you."

Diego smiled.

He had made an important decision.

"I'm not leaving, buddy,"

Diego said to Manny.

"All the adventure I want
is right here," said Diego.
"I couldn't leave my family."
Manny was glad
to have his friend back.
Everyone cheered with joy.
They were a family again!

The baby settled down for a nap.

She had two loving parents

and a big family of friends.

What more could a mammoth want?